W9-BXB-379

**from MISTY OF CHINCOTEAGUE by Marguerite Henry**

**excerpted and adapted by Joan Nichols**

**illustrated by Stephen Moore**

CHILDRENS PRESS CHOICE

A Checkerboard Press/Macmillan title selected for educational distribution

ISBN 0-516-09843-8

No one had ever captured the Phantom. She was the wildest member of the Pied Piper's band. She was also the smartest and the most beautiful. On Pony Penning Day when the wild ponies of Assateague Island were rounded up for the swim across the channel to Chincoteague, the Phantom always managed to escape.

"But this year will be different," Paul Beebe vowed.

"How Paul?" asked his sister, Maureen. "How will it be any different from last year or the year before?"

"Because this year, *I'm* riding in the roundup," Paul answered. "And *I'm* going to capture her!"

Paul and Maureen were on Assateague Island, hoping to catch a glimpse of the wild ponies.

"Look, Paul," Maureen whispered. "There they are."

"Do you see the Phantom, Paul?" Maureen asked.

"It's hard to tell," Paul answered. "They're all in a bunch."

Suddenly, as the children watched, one pony broke free and galloped off. The Pied Piper tore after her.

Paul's eyes widened in disbelief. "That's her!" In his excitement, he hardly breathed. "It's the Phantom."

Maureen hugged herself to keep from shouting. "She's beautiful."

The runaway Phantom was easy to recognize. Her coat was the color of copper. Silver streaked her mane and tail. Spread across her back was a strange white marking shaped like a map of the United States.

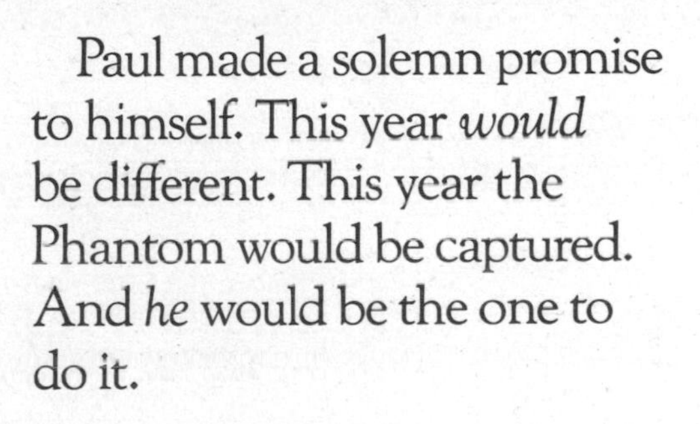

Paul made a solemn promise to himself. This year *would* be different. This year the Phantom would be captured. And *he* would be the one to do it.

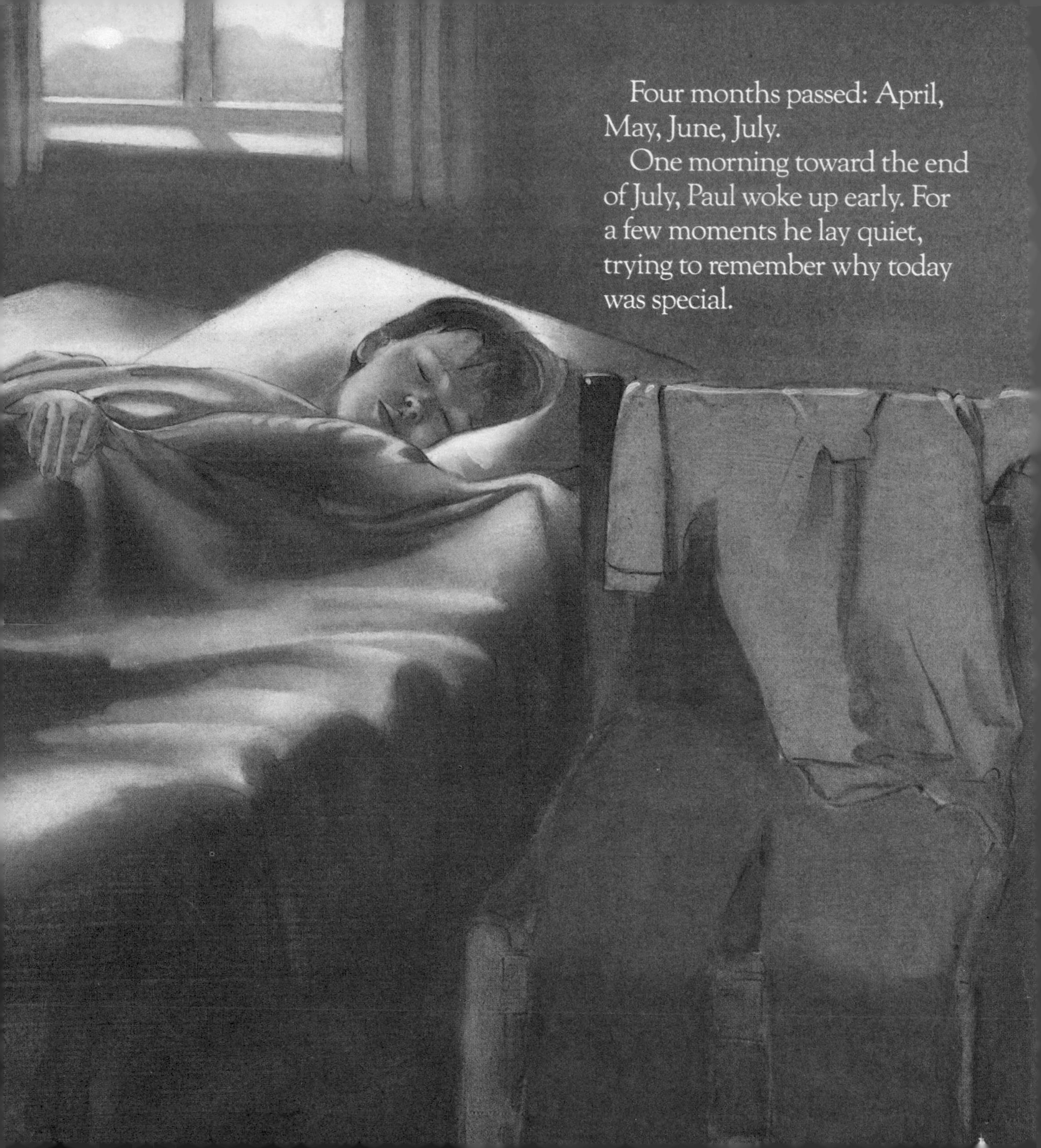

Four months passed: April, May, June, July.

One morning toward the end of July, Paul woke up early. For a few moments he lay quiet, trying to remember why today was special.

It was Pony Penning Day!

Paul leaped out of bed and grabbed for his clothes. Hurriedly, he pulled on his shirt and pants, then thudded downstairs to the kitchen.

“Good morning, Paul,” Grandma said. “Sit down and eat a breakfast fit for a roundup man!”

Feeling proud at being called a roundup man, Paul tried to eat. But he was so excited, the food just lumped in his throat.

He glanced at the clock. At last it was time. “I’ve got to go now,” he called and ran out the door.

Watch Eyes, a good, dependable pony, was waiting outside.

"Remember, Paul," Grandpa said, "obey your leader. No matter what."

Paul loped down the quiet streets of Chincoteague. Soon other roundup men joined him. In a few minutes they all clattered across the small bridge that led to Piney Island. There they boarded the old scow that would carry them across the channel to Assateague.

When they landed, they mounted their horses and turned to face their leader, Wyle Maddox.

"Split into three bunches," Wyle commanded, "and head north, south, and east." He motioned to Paul. "Paul, you and Kim Horsepepper come with me. We'll all meet at Tom's Point. Gee-up!"

Paul touched his bare heels to Watch Eye's sides. *They were off!*

Over pine woodlands and sand dunes, through marshes and mudholes they rode. Suddenly Wyle's horse reared into the air and neighed. About twenty yards ahead a band of wild ponies darted into the open, then vanished among the pines.

In a flash, Paul and the others gave chase, galloping as hard as they could. Paul was thrilled. Now he really felt like a roundup man!

Just then Wyle shouted, pointing. “Paul, there’s a straggler! Go after it!”

Paul was stunned. He wanted to go on whooping and hollering after the band of wild ponies, not chase after some puny pony that couldn't even keep up with the herd. He wanted to catch the Phantom!

Wyle Maddox wants to be rid of me, Paul thought. Maybe there isn't any straggler. Then he remembered Grandpa's words: "Obey your leader. No matter what."

With a sigh, he wheeled Watch Eyes into the pine thicket. His eyes swept the trees for the least sign of movement. He rode on, his body covered with sweat.

At last, far away and deep among the pines, something moved. It could have been anything—a deer, a squirrel. No matter, he was after it!

Suddenly Paul reined in. What was that in the bushes ahead? His heart beat wildly. There it was! A silver flash—like mist and sun. And just beyond, a glimpse of a long tail, the color of copper and silver.

"Could it be the Phantom?" Paul whispered. "It is! It is! It is! And the silver flash—it's a brand-new baby." The blood pounded in his ears. "No wonder the Phantom couldn't keep up with the herd," he murmured. "She has a baby!"

He, Paul Beebe, had done it. He had captured the Phantom!

But how was he going to get her and her misty little colt to Tom's Point to join up with the other ponies? Should he try driving them along the beach, or through the woods?

Just then the Pied Piper bugled through his nose, high quavering notes followed by a deep snorting rumble. It was almost as if he had commanded: "You get down here to Tom's Point. Now!"

Spinning around, the Phantom hurried off in his direction, her baby trotting along behind her.

Paul laughed. He didn't have to drive the Phantom and her colt to Tom's Point. They were leading him!